Published by BBC Books, a division of BBC Enterprises Limited,
Woodlands, 80 Wood Lane, London W12 0TT

First published in 1990

Edd the Duck © BBC Television 1990
Design, illustrations and text © Brainwaves Limited 1990

ISBN 0-563-36046-1

Printed in Singapore by Tien Wah Press (Pte.) Ltd

Edd the Duck
in Storyland

Devised by Christina Mackay-Robinson
Written by Keith Faulkner
Illustrated by Paul Johnson

BBC BOOKS

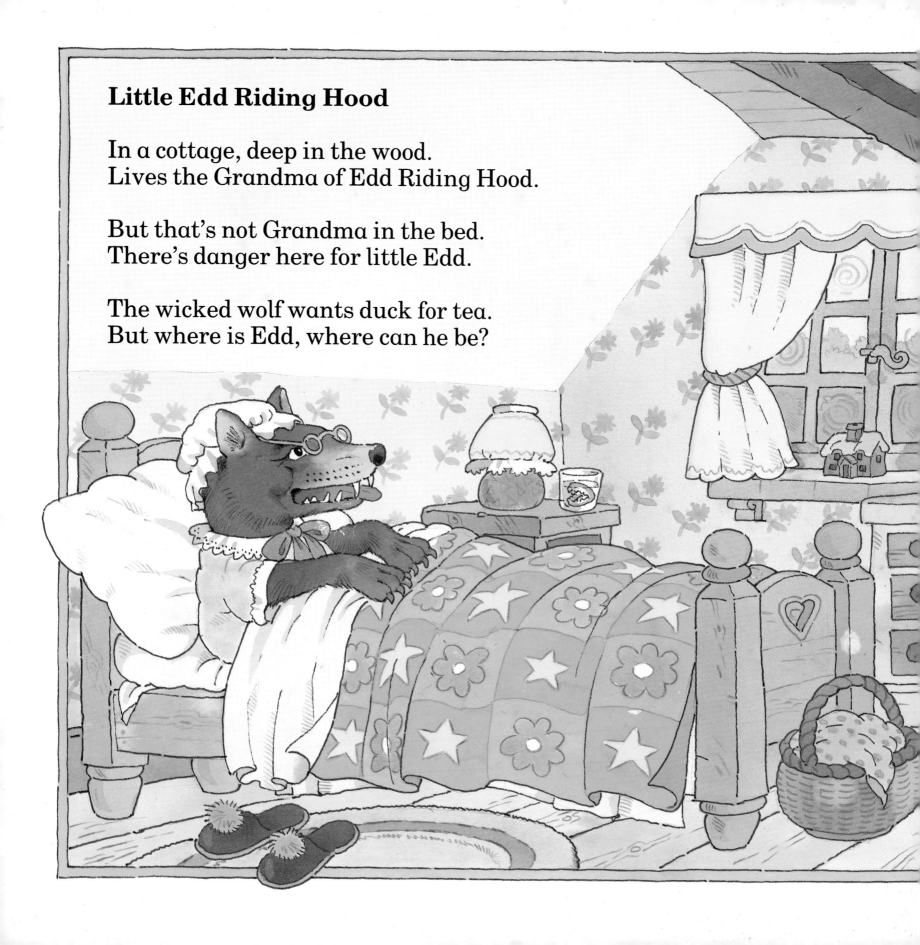

Little Edd Riding Hood

In a cottage, deep in the wood.
Lives the Grandma of Edd Riding Hood.

But that's not Grandma in the bed.
There's danger here for little Edd.

The wicked wolf wants duck for tea.
But where is Edd, where can he be?

Eddladdin

In a cave, as dark as night,
Aladdin's found some treasure bright.

He picks an old lamp from the dirt,
And rubs it hard upon his shirt.

A flash of light, what could it be?
Why don't you lift the flap and see?

Quack and the Beanstalk

Quack swopped a cow for a bean or two.
Now you can see how much they grew.

He ran away with the giant's goose.
Now the angry giant is on the loose.

The giant is looking very mean.
But, Quack is nowhere to be seen.

The Ugly Duckling

The mother swan looks on with pride,
But wait 'til she sees what's inside.

The last egg's rather oversized.
I think she's going to be surprised.

So, lift the flap and you will see.
How really cool a duck can be.

Edderella

The handsome prince has come to choose,
The one who fits the crystal shoes.

I think it comes as no surprise,
That these girls take a larger size.

Who fits the glass shoe on the floor?
Try peeping round the cellar door.

Duck Whittington

He came to London seeking fame.
Now everybody knows his name.

All he had was a faithful cat.
But now he wears the Lord Mayor's hat.

You'll find him up inside Big Ben.
Whose bells told him to turn again.

The Piedd Piper

The town of Hamelin's full of rats.
They've frightened off the dogs and cats.

But now it seems they're leaving soon.
All following the piper's tune.

Who could this clever piper be?
Why don't you lift the flap and see.

The Duck Prince

Down by the pond, the king's fair daughter,
Has dropped her ball into the water.

An ugly frog begins to tell,
That he's a prince changed by a spell.

One kiss will set the sad prince free.
Who could this frog prince really be?